SUPERBOOK®

IN THE
BEGINNING
THE STORY OF CREATION

Most Charisma House Book Group products are available at special quantity discounts for bulk purchase for sales promotions, premiums, fund-raising, and educational needs. For details, call us at (407) 333-0600 or visit our website at charismahouse.com.

Story adapted by Gwen Ellis et al. and published by Charisma House, 600 Rinehart Road, Lake Mary, Florida 32746

International Standard Book Number: 978-1-62999-844-2

This publication is translated in Spanish under the title *En el principio*, copyright © 2020 by The Christian Broadcasting Network, Inc. CBN.com; published by Casa Creación, a Charisma Media company. All rights reserved.

20 21 22 23 24 — 987654321

Printed in China

Chris and his robot, Gizmo, were standing outside of his father's lab when their friend Joy stopped by. Chris whispered, "Dad is working on a top secret project. I can't wait to find out what it is, but he won't let me in there!"

Suddenly the door burst open, and out came Chris's dad, Professor Quantum. "I've run out of magnets, and I can't finish my invention without them," he said. "I have to go buy some right now."

Then he looked Chris straight in the eye and warned, "Remember, Son—do not go into the lab. Is that clear?" And he rushed away.

Chris was surprised to see that the lab door was open. He was very curious—and very tempted. Guess what? Chris went in, with Joy and Gizmo right behind.

Inside was an amazing device. "Wow!" Chris exclaimed.

Joy asked, "What is it?"

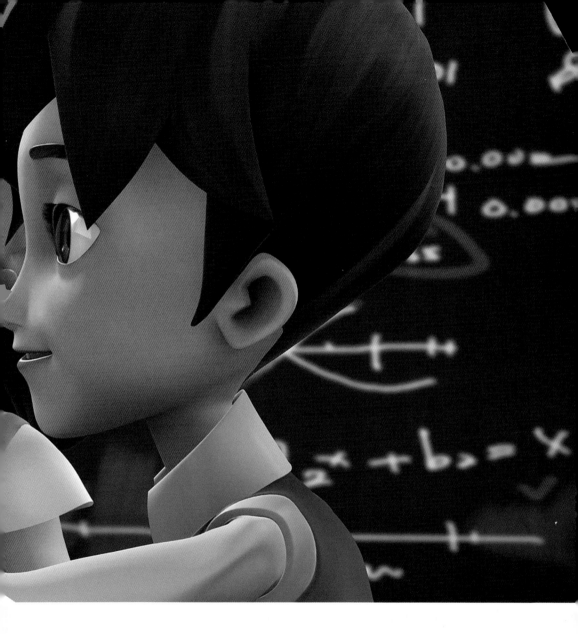

"My scanner says it is a personal jet pack with a totally new design," Gizmo reported.

"It probably wouldn't hurt if you just tried it on," Joy told Chris.

"No, stop!" Gizmo shouted. "Do not disobey your father."

But Chris ignored him and tried on his dad's fantastic invention. Suddenly the jet pack launched upward and took Chris for a wild ride, wrecking the lab. Then he crashed down with a thud—right in the middle of the big mess he had made.

"We need to clean this up," Chris groaned, "but there's no way we can do it before Dad gets home."

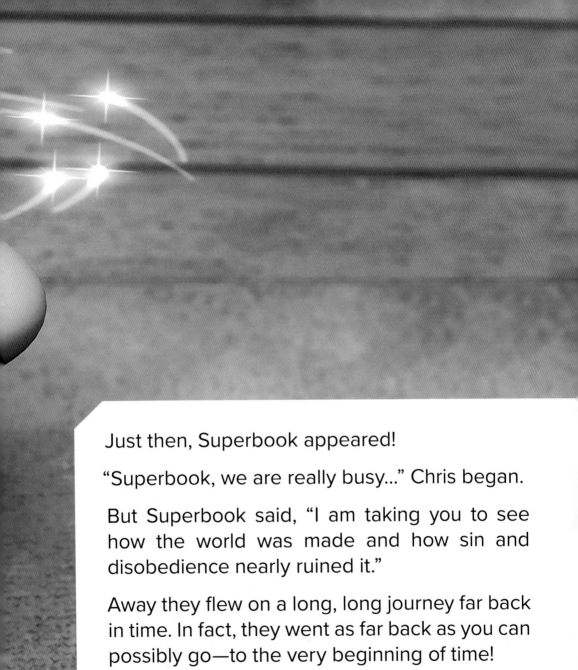

Just then, Superbook appeared!

"Superbook, we are really busy..." Chris began.

But Superbook said, "I am taking you to see how the world was made and how sin and disobedience nearly ruined it."

Away they flew on a long, long journey far back in time. In fact, they went as far back as you can possibly go—to the very beginning of time!

Darkness was everywhere. Then God commanded, "Let there be light!" And suddenly there was light!

He separated the water from the dry ground, where He made plants and trees to grow.

He created the sun, the moon, and all the stars in the sky.

Then the Lord made all types of fish and giant sea creatures that swim in the water.

God filled the skies with birds of every kind, and then He made the animals. Can you name some of your favorites? He created all of them—from little tiny creatures that creep very slowly to big wild beasts that run really fast!

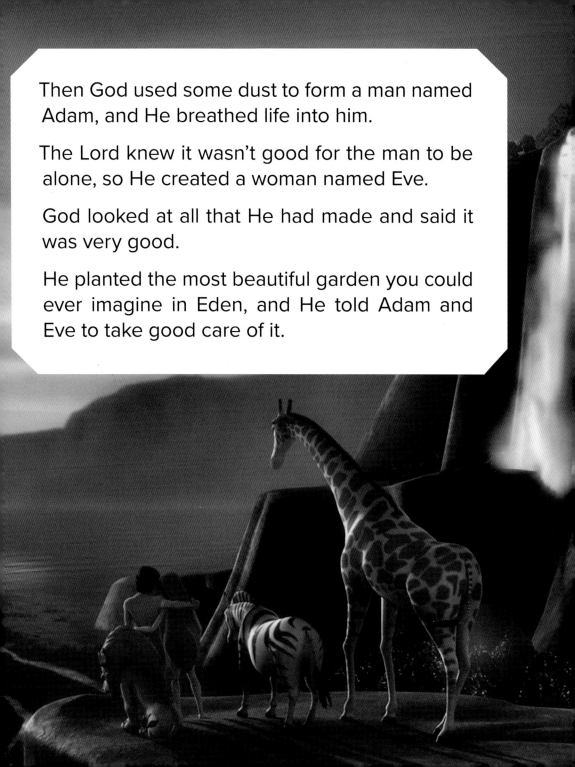

Then God used some dust to form a man named Adam, and He breathed life into him.

The Lord knew it wasn't good for the man to be alone, so He created a woman named Eve.

God looked at all that He had made and said it was very good.

He planted the most beautiful garden you could ever imagine in Eden, and He told Adam and Eve to take good care of it.

And that's when Chris, Joy, and Gizmo landed after their long journey through time.

"Where are we?" asked Chris.

"Eden," said a voice. The three travelers spun around to see Adam and Eve.

The couple explained that God had made this perfectly

beautiful, perfectly happy place.

Even the wild animals were perfectly friendly! The children were amazed to see that there was no sadness or sickness anywhere.

"God has given us everything we could ever need right here," Eve told them.

Adam added, "We may enjoy it all, except we must not eat from the tree of the knowledge of good and evil."

"Why is eating that fruit a problem?" Gizmo asked.

"God wants what is best for us," Eve explained. "That's why

we need to do whatever He asks. Anything else would be—"

"Disobedience," Joy chimed in.

Suddenly Chris remembered how he had disobeyed his father's warning not to go into the lab.

One day Eve met an amazing creature. It looked a little like a snake and a little like a lizard because it had legs—and it could talk!

But what that serpent said was not good, because it was God's enemy.

You see, an angel named Lucifer had rebelled against God long ago. Lucifer thought he knew better than the Lord!

God had thrown him out of heaven because of his pride and disobedience. But Lucifer was still fighting against God, and that's why he went to Eden disguised as a serpent.

That evil serpent wanted Eve to doubt God, so he asked, "Did God really say you must not eat fruit from any trees in the garden?"

She said, "It's only the fruit from the tree in the middle of the garden that we are not allowed to eat—or we will die."

"Oh, you won't die!" the serpent hissed. "God knows that your eyes will be opened as soon as you eat it, and you will

be like God, knowing both good and evil."

Eve was convinced! The fruit looked delicious, and she just had to try it. So she did! Then she gave some to Adam, who was with her—and he ate it too!

Uh-oh. Now what would happen?

That evening, God came to talk with Adam and Eve as He usually did. But this time, He could not find them.

"Where are you?" God called.

They came out of hiding wearing fig leaves. Adam said, "I was afraid because I was naked, so I hid."

The Lord asked, "Who told you that you were naked? Have you eaten the fruit I commanded you not to eat?"

Well, Adam blamed Eve, and then Eve blamed the serpent for tricking her.

God punished the serpent by making it crawl on its belly. And He disciplined Adam and Eve by putting them out of the garden. "We have lost Eden," Eve cried.

How sad! Sin and disobedience had come into the world. So had sickness, pain, and death.

Yet all was not lost forever, because God had a wonderful plan for the future. And so He promised Eve that sin, evil, and death would be defeated by one of her descendants someday!

That's when Superbook took the three friends back to the lab—just as Professor Quantum walked in the door and saw the big mess!

"What happened here?" he asked sternly.

"It's my fault," Chris admitted. "I'm really sorry."

"I forgive you," said his dad. "But there are consequences when you disobey. You can't go to the skateboard park for a month, and you must clean up the whole lab."

Chris nodded slowly and asked, "Dad, do you still love me?"

"Yes," said his father with a smile. "I will always love you." And he gave his son a good long hug.

"For I know the plans I have for you," says the LORD. "They are plans for good and not for disaster, to give you a future and a hope."

—Jeremiah 29:11